Greetings. I am Master Wu. I am here to tell you about my students, the Secret Ninja Force.

This is the story of how they defeated one enemy, but found a new challenge.

The Secret Ninja Force has six members – Lloyd, Nya, Cole, Jay, Kai and Zane. They are high school students, and they also protect Ninjago City. They are very busy teenagers!

Scholastic Children's Books,
Euston House, 24 Eversholt Street,
London NW1 1DB, UK

A division of Scholastic Ltd
London ~ New York ~ Toronto ~ Sydney ~ Auckland
Mexico City ~ New Delhi ~ Hong Kong

First published in the US by Scholastic Inc, 2017, as two titles:
High-Tech Ninja Heroes
Lord Garmadon, Evil Dad
This edition published in the UK by Scholastic Ltd, 2017

Adapted by Michael Petranek from the screenplay

Story by Hillary Winston & Bob Logan & Paul Fisher and Bob Logan & Paul Fisher & William Wheeler & Tom Wheeler

Screenplay by Bob Logan & Paul Fisher & William Wheeler & Tom Wheeler and Jared Stern & John Whittington

Book design by Jessica Meltzer

ISBN 978 1407 18461 6

Printed in Slovakia by TBB

2 4 6 8 10 9 7 5 3 1

Papers used by Scholastic Children's Books are made from wood grown in sustainable forests.

HIGH-TECH NINJA HEROES

ADAPTED BY MICHAEL PETRANEK FROM THE SCREENPLAY

STORY BY HILARY WINSTON & BOB LOGAN & PAUL FISHER AND BOB LOGAN &
PAUL FISHER & WILLIAM WHEELER & TOM WHEELER

SCREENPLAY BY BOB LOGAN & PAUL FISHER & WILLIAM WHEELER &
TOM WHE_____NITTINGTON

Ninjago City's biggest enemy is Lord Garmadon. Garmadon has four arms, red eyes, sharp teeth and … he's my brother.
Most of our family get-togethers are not very fun.

Garmadon is the head of an army of Sharkmen. In truth, they are not actually Sharkmen – just men and women wearing shark suits. They can attack Ninjago City from the water.

Lloyd is the Green Ninja, and he leads the Secret Ninja Force. Lloyd builds all the ninja's mechs too.

Garmadon is Lloyd's dad, but they are not very close. Garmadon pronounces his name wrong – he calls him "La-loyd". But the first *L* is supposed to be silent, like a ninja.

Koko is Lloyd's mother. She has always told Lloyd she and Garmadon worked in an office together before he decided to take over the world. He was much friendlier back then.

Kai and Nya are brother and sister. Kai is fearless and hot-headed, while Nya is one of the best students I have ever taught.

Cole is another member of the ninja team. He loves music. His mech has an awesome sound system, and he loves making mix tapes. If you don't know what that is, ask an older person.

Jay is the Blue Ninja, and he is a great inventor. He loves to tell jokes and is very hard-working.

Zane is a Nindroid who is always trying to fit in and crack jokes, but being a robot makes him a little different.

The ninja all have cool mechs that they use to fight anyone who invades Ninjago City...

The mechs are cool, but it takes more than technology to be a true ninja. Ninja are sneaky. These mechs are very, very loud!

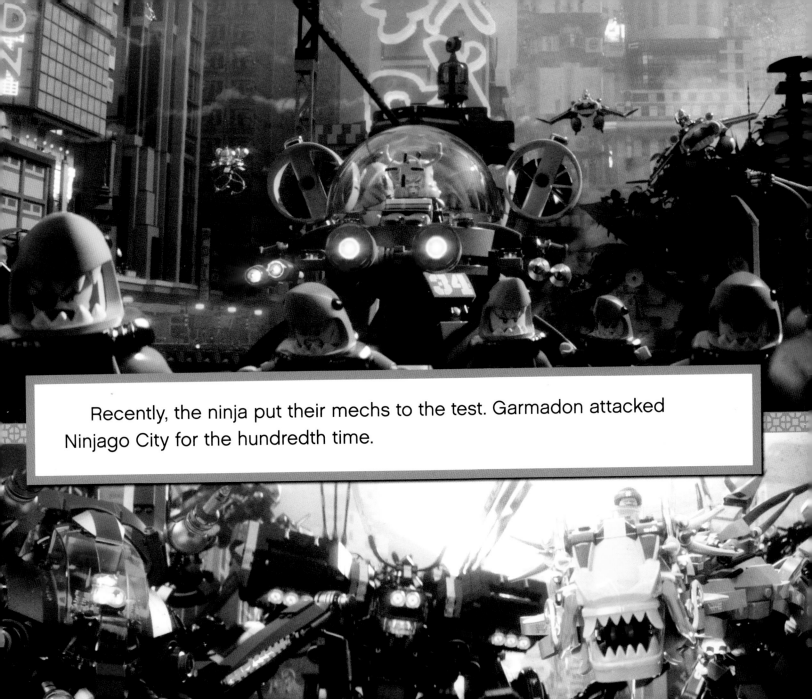

Recently, the ninja put their mechs to the test. Garmadon attacked Ninjago City for the hundredth time.

The ninja are very good at protecting the city, but sometimes they end up causing a lot of damage.

During the battle, Lloyd fell off his mech and landed in an apartment. He had to protect a baby while fighting some Sharkmen. He had his hands full!

The ninja defeated Garmadon and sent him back to his volcano lair.
"I'll be back," Garmadon vowed. "And when I return, I'll have something
really wicked for you!"

I knew what Garmadon said was true. He would be back, and things would only get worse.

We returned to the ship where I train the ninja, the *Destiny's Bounty*. Lloyd, Nya, Cole, Jay, Kai and Zane were very happy they'd defeated Garmadon.

"Guys, that was awesome! Today we were so ninja!" Nya said.

But I had some things I needed to tell the ninja.

"There's nothing *ninja* about you," I said. "Ninja are supposed to be invisible! But you keep blowing everything up with your crazy machines!

"Garmadon will be back, same as before," I said. "Some day you will come up against something your mechs cannot beat. It is time to truly become … ninja!"

I know the ninja were disappointed. They did not want to listen to me, but it was true. They needed to become *real* ninja. Not just crazy kids with wacky mechs.

So we began training. And it is here that you find us.

Garmadon will come back, and when he does, the ninja must find their inner strength and become true ninja. For that is the only way they will ever defeat him and save Ninjago City for good!

So now that I know my kid's the Green Ninja, I need a new plan to conquer Ninjago City. I've got to put my kid in his place. I mean, I might be an evil warlord, but I'm still his dad!

And Daddy's got a plan that La-Lloyd will never see coming. Ha, ha, ha!

The Secret Ninja Force members are probably training, getting ready for me to come back. I mean, hey, I always come back! I love destroying stuff with my crazy machines.

I heard a tired voice on the other end. "It's Lloyd. Your son."

"La-Lloyd?" I asked. "I must have pocket-dialed you." I hung up. I needed to think of new ways to defeat the Secret Ninja Force, not spend time on the phone with my kid!

But it was good to know I had his phone number.

I guess I must have put my phone in my back pocket, because suddenly I heard a voice talking to me.

"Hello?" I asked. "Who's this?"

We turned and headed back to our lair.

I couldn't believe my kid was the Green Ninja. I needed some serious "me" time. I had to think about what I should do next...

"Pfft. No, it's L-L-O-Y-D — La-Lloyd. I named you," I said. "And that's not true — I haven't even been a part of your life. How could I ruin it? I wasn't even there."

I couldn't believe it! It was La-Lloyd!

"That's right. It's me, your son. And it's *Lloyd*," he said. "You ruined my life, Dad."

I stared down the Secret Ninja Force.

"I'll be back," I said. "And you better be ready for me to conquer Ninjago City!"

That's when the Green Ninja spoke up. "Oh, I'll be waiting ... Dad..."

But it turned out their high-tech mechs were slightly more high-tech than my high-tech mechs, so...
Anyway, the battle didn't quite go the way I wanted. We were toast.

It was the Secret Ninja Force! And they had vehicles too! Big mechs.
That wasn't good news for us. Still, we kept on fighting.

I was enjoying watching my Shark Army petrify all the people in the city. But suddenly, things started to be not so fun. I heard a lot of noise – and it was way louder than the usual noise of taking over the city.

The people were pretty stunned. See that hot dog guy? Stunned. That's what happens when the most evil guy of all time takes over your city in less time than it takes to put mustard on a hot dog.

... and then my Shark Army used their mechs to storm the city from the sea. We were all over Ninjago City in no time!

All those mechs and awesome shark costumes came in handy when I decided to attack Ninjago City for the millionth time. It just never gets old to me! We started by flying into the city...

We've got cool vehicles too. Crabs, birds, you name it. We can crawl, fly or swim right into your city.

That's just what we did during our most recent adventure...

My brother may have his own team of ninja, but I've got something even better – a Shark Army! Take that, ninja nerds!

So yeah, the Secret Ninja Force. They're a bunch of high school kids who don't want me to have any fun or conquer Ninjago City. The Green Ninja is their leader.

Did my family support me? No. You see, I've got a brother named Master Wu, and he trains that Secret Ninja Force.

If you've got a brother or a sister who won't share toys with you, trust me, it could be worse. My brother trains a group of high school kids to fight me! I mean, what's up with that?

This is me and La-Lloyd's mum, Koko. There was a time when I wasn't so evil. Koko and I were a couple before I decided to just go for the whole evil lord thing.

Koko likes to tell people I tried doing an office job for a while, but it wasn't the right fit. So I decided to be a full-time bad guy.

I've got a son, but he's not evil like his old man. La-Lloyd is his name. I just learned that he's also the leader of the Secret Ninja Force. I've been fighting the Green Ninja for a while now – never knew he was my kid!

More on that later...

So like I said, I'm a bad guy ... but not just any bad guy. I've been called the baddest guy ever in the history of Ninjago City.

Whoa, look at me! I look cool. Not bad!

Hey there. Garmadon checking in. Lord Garmadon, that is. I've got four arms and pointy teeth and I'm pretty much all about conquering Ninjago City. It's been a dream of mine for a while. And I'm pretty close to achieving it.

But first, here's more about me...

Scholastic Children's Books,
Euston House, 24 Eversholt Street,
London NW1 1DB, UK

A division of Scholastic Ltd
London ~ New York ~ Toronto ~ Sydney ~ Auckland
Mexico City ~ New Delhi ~ Hong Kong

First published in the US by Scholastic Inc, 2017, as two titles:
High-Tech Ninja Heroes
Lord Garmadon, Evil Dad
This edition published in the UK by Scholastic Ltd, 2017

Adapted by Michael Petranek from the screenplay

Story by Hillary Winston & Bob Logan & Paul Fisher and Bob Logan & Paul Fisher & William Wheeler & Tom Wheeler

Screenplay by Bob Logan & Paul Fisher & William Wheeler & Tom Wheeler and Jared Stern & John Whittington

Book design by Jessica Meltzer

ISBN 978 1407 18461 6

MIX
From responsible
sources
FSC® C022120

Printed in Slovakia by TBB

2 4 6 8 10 9 7 5 3 1

Papers used by Scholastic Children's Books are made from wood grown in sustainable forests.

THE LEGO NINJAGO MOVIE

LORD GARMADON, EVIL DAD

ADAPTED BY MICHAEL PETRANEK
FROM THE SCREENPLAY

STORY BY HILARY WINSTON &
BOB LOGAN & PAUL FISHER AND
BOB LOGAN & PAUL FISHER &
WILLIAM WHEELER & TOM WHEELER

SCREENPLAY BY BOB LOGAN &
PAUL FISHER & WILLIAM WHEELER &
TOM WHEELER AND JARED STERN &
JOHN WHITTINGTON

SCHOLASTIC